MW00902142

To Rowan Ella Vicory

who has a compassionate spirit

like "Young Noah" :)

Merry Christmas 2020

Love, Gramma + Grandpa

Vicory

YOUNG NOAH

A LAMB'S TALE

FORWARD

THE IDEA FOR THIS BOOK INITIALLY CAME ABOUT IN THE EARLY 2000'S.
I APPROACHED ERIC (THE AUTHOR) ABOUT A YOUNG NOAH BOOK SERIES AND AFTER MANY YEARS, DELAYS AND SIDE ROADS, YOUNG NOAH WAS BORN.

HAVING ATTENDED GRAD SCHOOL AND OBTAINING A DEGREE IN MENTAL HEALTH COUNSELING, I WAS CONTINUALLY REMINDED OF MY OWN STRUGGLES WITH DYSLEXIA AND ADHD WHICH GREATLY AFFECTED MY ABILITY TO LEARN.

THE TREMENDOUS FEAR AND TOXIC SHAME I SUFFERED ASSOCIATED WITH SCHOLASTIC DIFFICULTIES AND EMBARRASSING SOCIAL INTERACTION DROVE ME TO EXCESSIVE PARTYING IN MY TEEN YEARS TO COPE WITH THE PAIN.

GOD IN HIS MERCY INTERVENED IN THE MIDST OF MY HARDEST STRUGGLES AND REVEALED HIS LOVE AND PLAN OF SALVATION TO ME THROUGH HIS SON YESHUA (JESUS) AT 21 YEARS OF AGE.

FROM FIRSTHAND EXPERIENCE, I REALIZED THAT YOUNG CHILDREN SOMETIMES HAVE GREAT DIFFICULTY EXPRESSING STRONG NEGATIVE FEELINGS ABOUT WHAT THEY ARE BATTLING WITH. YOUNG NOAH'S PURPOSE, I BELIEVE, IS TO BRING CHILDREN ENGAGING STORIES OF CONQUERING FEARS AND DISABILITY STIGMAS THROUGH THE CHALLENGED ANIMALS HELPED BY YOUNG NOAH.

YOUNG NOAH, IMAGINED AS A CHILD HIMSELF, IS DIVINELY GIFTED TO SEE AND SOLVE EACH ANIMAL'S DILEMMA THROUGH FOCUSSED PROBLEM-SOLVING AND INSPIRED INSIGHT.

APPROACHING PROBLEMS FROM DIFFERENT PERSPECTIVES, HEALING THROUGH COMPASSIONATE UNDERSTANDING AND EMBRACING TRUTH IS THE HALLMARK OF THIS PLANNED BOOK SERIES.

C W PARRY MA   MARCH 2019

YOUNG NOAH
A LAMB'S TALE

Copyright 2019 by Eric McConnell
All rights reserved. No part of this book may be used or reprodused in any manner whatsoever without written permission (excluding featured Bible scripture verses) except in the case of brief quotations embodied in critical articles or reviews.
Thank you for buying an authorized edition of this book and for complying with copyright laws by not reproducing, scanning or distributing any part of it in any form without permission.

For information contact:
Eric McConnell **WWW.EMPSTORYBOARDS.COM**
Written and illustrated by
Eric McConnell Story idea by CW Parry MA
Cover and interior design by Eric McConnell with Ron Lucarelli

ISBN: 978-0-578-48113-5 (hardcover)
Library of Congress Catalogue-In-Publishing Data is available
Printed in the United States of America
10 9 8 7 6 65 4 3 2 1
First Edition: March 2019

YOUNG NOAH

A LAMB'S TALE

WRITTEN AND ILLLUSTRATED BY

ERIC MCCONNELL

STORY / IDEA BY

CW PARRY, MA

BUT JESUS CALLED THE CHILDREN TO HIM AND SAID, "LET THE LITTLE CHILDREN COME TO ME, AND DO NOT HINDER THEM, FOR THE KINGDOM OF GOD BELONGS TO SUCH AS THESE" -LUKE 18:16 NIV

A LAMB'S TALE

Many thousands of years ago when the world was bright and green, lived a young boy named Noah.

He and his family made their home out in the country away from the city and tended their farm. They grew vegetables but also raised sheep.

Noah was a shepherd boy who helped his father care for the sheep.

As with other mornings, Noah and his father Lamech walked the short distance from their family's house in the cliffs to the nearby grassy field where their sheep grazed.

It was late spring nearing summer and lambs which had been born several months earlier were frolicking in the field everywhere. They loved to run and leap and race each other. It was so much fun to see. One little lamb could not join them, however, but only watch

from the sideline because his hind leg
was lame and shorter than his other
legs. He tried to run, but couldn't
keep up with the other lambs.

The lambs bullied and teased him about
it.

"Ha ha! Limpy-Leg can't catch us!" They'd
taunt.
It made the little lamb very sad as he
looked at his lame leg.

Being depressed and embarrassed that
he was being teased, the little lamb
teared up.
The other lambs all laughed at him.

Noah saw him crying. Noah had a special ability (*a gift) to understand what animals said and felt. The animals came to him with their problems and though not speaking to him, Noah

understood what they were trying to tell him. The animals sensed this about him and would come to him with their struggles and pain.

Noah had seen what happened and went over to the downcast little lamb.

"What's wrong, little lamb? Can I help you?" Asked Noah.

The teary-eyed little lamb looked up at Noah and Noah immediately knew what was going on as he glanced at the lamb's leg.

"My hind leg is shorter than my other legs. I try to run after the others as fast as I can, but can't keep up. Then they tease me and make fun of me. Why are they so mean?" The lamb seemed to say.

"Oh little lamb- I am so sorry they were so mean to you! Let me see if I can think of something to help you run better. I'll be right back!" Said Noah. Noah knew in his heart it was best to ask God, the Creator of everything what he should do.

He knew he didn't have the answer within himself.

Noah loved to go to what he called his "quiet place"- a beautiful re-treat into the forest next to a stream. God would meet him there and speak quietly into his heart.
Noah prayed while on his way there:

"Lord God, please help me to figure out what to do for the little lamb. He's so sad, down and depressed!"

When Noah arrived at his favorite place in the forest next to a gentle stream, he sat down on a large fallen tree trunk to think and ponder.

A colorful talkative parrot named Java often joined him there, sitting next to him on the tree trunk while chattering away.

Speaking out loud to himself (*do you ever do that?) he wondered, "How can I fix that little lamb's leg so he can run and play with the others?"

Discouraged, Noah sat there without a clue of what to do.

Suddenly, "Why don't you build him a
special wheel?" said an unseen voice.
"What? Who said that?" Noah nervously
called out.
"Up here! Up here!" The soft voice
replied.

Noah turned around and looked behind him. Scared, Java jumped off the tree trunk and flew up into the air.

Above his shoulder towered a young dragon who'd blended into the background eating tree leaves and whom Noah hadn't noticed earlier. Before the modern term "dinosaur" existed, the large creatures were called dragons.

Noah was dumbfounded. Rarely had he ever seen a dragon and even then only from a distance, because dragons were feared by people.

"My name's Bronnie! What's yours?" the young female dragon said.   "I overheard you and thought that maybe I could help with your problem, be-cause I have a different view than you do."

"Y-y-youu can SPEAK?" An amazed Noah asked.

"Yes, when we want to. Unlike the other animals which can't." Explained Bronnie.

"W-w-what do you think I should do?" Noah replied to Bronnie- still stunned.

Why don't you make a wooden brace for the lamb's leg, which could be fastened to it with a leather wrap?

Then, mount a wheel at the end of the brace, so his leg could be the same length as his others and roll as he runs!" offered Bronnie.

Noah was astonished at the young dragon's idea. He knew dragons lived many hundreds of years and though fierce, possessed wisdom.

Still somewhat scared, Noah now realized that God had heard him and had
answered his prayer- though in a way
he didn't expect.

Java the parrot landed back on Noah's
shoulder, peering around the side of
his head at Bronnie.

"You can make the brace as a pole
slightly longer than the lamb's leg.
It can be made out of a strong branch
of Acacia wood, the same as your
staff, found here in the forest."
Added Bronnie.

"That's a great idea!" exclaimed Noah. "I'll get the wood, go home and build it! Thank you, Bronnie!"

"You're welcome! Could I come and watch the lamb run when it's finished?" Asked Bronnie.

"Sure!" said an excited Noah. "Do you know where the pasture is?"

"Yes. I like to spend time there when no one's around." Said Bronnie.

Before going home to build the brace, Noah returned to the sheep pasture and put the little lamb on his shoulders, carrying it back to his workshop.

Noah had always enjoyed working with wood.

As the lamb watched, he measured, cut and finished the wooden pole to be used as the brace. Drilling a hole through it's end, he attached a round-carved piece of
wood as a wheel with an axle. The axle and wheel were held in place with wooden pins.

Noah fastened the brace to the lamb's leg with a leather wrap and straps.

It fit comfortably and the little lamb found it much easier to walk as he and Noah returned to the pasture.

When they arrived, the little lamb looked out at the other lambs frolicking and hestitated, looking up at Noah.

"Go on! Go on- give it a try! You were moving so easily on our walk back to the pasture! I'll be right here watching you!" Encouraged Noah.

So the little lamb trotted out to meet the other lambs but then- broke into a run and galloped right through them!

Noah couldn't believe what he was seeing.

The other lambs didn't know what to think. This lamb they had teased, bullied and picked on because of his physical challenge now had blazed past them like a comet! They gave chase.

Well ahead, the lamb cut sharply
around a large rock and hid there.
The other lambs ran right past- never
seeing him.

When they finally turned around, there the little lamb was, grinning and laughing at THEM! Ha! Ha!

He took off like a flash in the opposite direction- running so fast with his newly-fixed leg that the other lambs couldn't keep up.

As an amazed Noah looked on, the little lamb found that he not only ran fast, but cut corners sharply and out-manuevered the other lambs easily.

The lambs ran as fast as they could, trying to keep up with the little lamb but kept falling behind.

Noah was overjoyed and cheered him on.

By now, Bronnie had joined Noah at the pasture and together they watched the little lamb sprinting home down the final stretch.

Noah was overjoyed and threw his arms around the victorious little lamb as the other lambs looked on.

"Way to go, little lamb- you did great! I'm so proud of you! But you need a name. I'm going to call you Ramsey!"

The little lamb was pleased.

Bronnie smiled a big smile.

"Can you believe it? He beat us!"
Wow, can HE run!" "We shouldn't have
teased him like that!" "That was
wrong." the lambs exclaimed.
Noah brought the little lamb Ramsey
back to his sheep-parents, who were
thrilled with his newly-fixed leg.

Noah related the incredible story of all that had happened and how his prayer to God had been answered, sharing with his father as they walked home from the pasture.

acknowledgements

FOR THE INVALUABLE CONTRIBUTIONS TO THE WRITING AND PUTTING TOGETHER OF THIS BOOK, I WANT TO FIRST THANK MY MOM AND DAD, GERALDINE AND GEORGE MC CONNELL.
BOTH ARTISTS THEMSELVES, THEY CONTINUALLY ENCOURAGED MY CREATIVE PROCESS AND PURSUITS THROUGHOUT CHILDHOOD AND MY LIFE.
BOTH GIFTED PAINTERS, I GREATLY ADMIRED THEIR LEVEL OF SKILL AND SOUGHT TO EMULATE THEM FROM AN EARLY AGE.

MY CLOSE FRIEND CRAIG PARRY, WHO ORIGINATED THE IDEA OF YOUNG NOAH IN THE EARLY 2000'S AND CONVINCED ME TO PURSUE THE CHARACTER AND STORYLINE POSSIBILITIES.

LIKE ME, CRAIG ENDURED MORE THAN HIS SHARE OF OSTRACISM, RIDICULE AND REJECTION. THIS INSPIRED HIM TO BECOME A MENTAL HEALTH COUNSELOR AND HELP OTHERS IN THEIR BATTLE WITH THE SAME STRUGGLES. HIS CONTRIBUTION TO THE CORE OF THIS BOOK'S CONTENT MADE IT POSSIBLE.

THANKS TO MY DEAR FRIEND VICTORIA TAYLOR ,WHO'S CONSISTENT ENCOURAGEMENT HELPED ME MOVE FORWARD WITH THIS PROJECT IN GENUINE FAITH.

THANKS AND GRATITUDE ALSO GO TO RON LUCARELLI- A GOOD FRIEND AND GIFTED GRAPHIC DESIGNER WHO TOOK MY HACK DIGITAL COVER DESIGN EFFORTS TO THE NEXT LEVEL. WITHOUT HIS CALM SPIRIT AND YEARS OF EXPERIENCE, THIS BOOK WOULD STILL BE SITTING ON MY COMPUTER'S HARD DRIVE.

FINALLY, I WANT TO THANK MY LORD AND SAVIOR JESUS CHRIST, WHO GAVE HIS LIFE FOR ME THAT I COULD TRULY KNOW GOD AND HIS INCREDIBLE LOVE FOR ME. HE IS THE SOURCE OF THE INSPIRATION FOR THE YOUNG NOAH STORIES AND THEIR INTENDED PURPOSE FOR HELPING CHILDREN EVERYWHERE COPE WITH LIFE'S CHALLENGES.

CPSIA information can be obtained
at www.ICGtesting.com
Printed in the USA
LVHW070504121020
668549LV00016B/347

* 9 7 8 0 5 7 8 4 8 1 1 3 5 *